The Naughty Fairy's

NAUGHTY SURPRISE

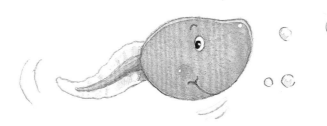

Nick Ward

little bee

In a quiet corner
of the palace gardens,
deep in a still green pond,
a little tadpole popped
out of his egg...

POP!

"**Wow!**"
he gasped
as he saw all the wonderful
creatures swimming around him.

"What will I be
when I grow up?"

But just then a passing princess
scooped him up.
"Are you my handsome prince?"
she asked, giving him a kiss.

"Oh dear,"
said the little
frog, feeling
another change
coming on...

"I'm a handsome prince!" he cried, and was just about to give the princess another kiss, when...

WHOOOSH!

A naughty fairy grabbed the princess and whisked her away to a tall rickety tower.

"Help!" she cried. "Save me!"

So the handsome prince ran through the woods
and over a mountain, till he came to the tall rickety tower.
But two ugly trolls were guarding the tower.

"**Gnarr!**" they roared, scrunching
up their faces.

"That's not scary," said
the handsome prince.

And he pulled such horrible faces that the trolls screamed and ran away!

So the handsome prince rescued the princess, which turned him into a...

Hero! "You're my hero!" sighed the princess, and the hero quickly marched the Big Bad Wolf and some big bully giants out of town.

(That was a hero's job, you see.)

"And don't come back till you're sorry!" he ordered.

The princess was so grateful to him for making
her country safe that she decided to marry her hero.
And this turned him into a rich and powerful...

King! He was a kind and considerate king and was loved by all his subjects, right down to the lowliest pig farmer. They lived in a beautiful palace and were very happy together.

Soon the king and queen had a baby daughter,
and this turned the king into a...

Daddy! "Yippee, I'm a daddy!"
He was so excited that he held a huge
party.

Everyone was invited:
the Three Bears,

the Three Little Pigs and

Little Red Riding Hood.

Everyone except the naughty fairy!

The naughty fairy was so annoyed that she
wrapped a naughty magic spell in a box, and tied
a beautiful bow on top. "I'll teach him!" she grumbled.

The naughty fairy put on a disguise
and took her present to the king...

"**Congratulations!**" she cackled.
But the king recognized the fairy
and guessed it was a trick.

Toot!
Toot!

Squeak!

"I can't undo the bow," he pretended.
"Oh, give it here, silly!" said the naughty fairy.

And she ripped off the paper and opened the box.

"Oh no!"

The magic spell whizzed around the fairy's head and -POP!
she disappeared.

POP!

"Where has she gone?" cried the king.

In a quiet corner of the palace
gardens, deep in a still green
pond, a naughty little tadpole
gasped at all the wonderful creatures.

POP!

"What will I be
when I grow up?"

she wondered...

For Peter and Hazel.
Beware of Naughty Fairies!

N.W.

First published in 2006
by Meadowside Children's Books
This edition published 2010 by Little Bee,
an imprint of Meadowside Children's Books
185 Fleet Street, London, EC4A 2HS
Text and illustrations © Nick Ward 2006

The right of Nick Ward to be identified as the
author and illustrator of this work has been
asserted by him in accordance with the Copyright,
Designs and Patents Act, 1988

A CIP catalogue record for this book
is available from the British Library
Printed in China
10 9 8 7 6 5 4 3 2